DONALD NEILSON

In 1975, 17 year-old Lesley Whittle was abducted by a callous killer whose sinister appearance earned him the nickname of the Black Panther. For Lesley, the kidnap ended in unimaginable horror. Eleven months were to pass before the Panther was finally cornered.

Express & Star, Wolverhampton

ONE

KIDNAP

The Night Intruder

Using stealth and meticulous advance planning, the Black Panther broke into a house in the village of Highley and kidnapped a schoolgirl called Lesley Whittle. It was the beginning of an 11 month manhunt.

On the evening of 13 January 1975, Lesley Whittle went to bed early. Lesley, a 17 year-old student, lived with her mother on the main street of the village of Highley in Shropshire. Lesley's mother returned home at 1.30 a.m. and, before going to bed, she went to check on her daughter. Lesley was asleep in her bedroom.

Soon after that, during the small hours of 14 January, a sinister figure approached the house, clad head-to-toe in black and wearing a hood with slits for eyes and mouth. Working silently and expertly, he cut the telephone wires that provided contact with the outside world, and then forced his way inside the house via the garage. Passing through the lounge, he went straight to Lesley's bedroom.

Abduction

Lesley Whittle was woken with a rough shake. A figure, of small but athletic build, was standing by her bed pointing a sawn-off shotgun between her eyes. He left her in no doubt that he would kill her if she failed to follow instructions.

Putting tape over her mouth, the black-clad figure led Lesley downstairs and outside to a green Morris. He bound her wrists and ankles and placed tape over her eyes before laying her down in the rear seat.

Retracing his steps, he went back into the lounge and left a coil of plastic Dymo tape, which he had prepared earlier, with three ransom messages printed on it.

Returning to the car, Lesley's abductor removed his hood and put on an ordinary jacket, placing his holdall bag with his house-breaking tools in the boot. He then set off on the

BACKGROUND

The wealthy [illegible]'s £2 wife

By FRANK GOLDSWORTHY

£106,000 WILL SHOCK FOR WOMAN WHO LIVED 30 YEARS 'CHEEK BY JOWL' WITH POVERTY

AT last, now he is dead, the riches of ex-bus driver George Whittle will help to make life easier for the estranged wife to whom for nearly 30 years he never paid more than £2 a week separation money. He always declared he could not afford to increase the allowance, Mrs. Selena Whittle said yesterday.

But when George Whittle died in 1970, aged 65, she read in a local newspaper that he had left £106,000.

That, a High Court judge was told, was only part of the fortune Mr. Whittle built up from a family coach business at Highley, near Bridgnorth, Shropshire.

BLONDE

Earlier he had given £70,000, a house and two properties bringing in £1,200 a year rent to 55-year-old Mrs. Dorothy Whittle.

She came into his life as a 25-year-old blonde he met on his bus.

Eventually they lived together, she changed her name to Whittle and

DOROTHY WHITTLE

RONALD WHITTLE

A DETAIL FROM THE OVERLORD TAPESTRY

D-Day tapestry goes on show

PART of a tapestry showing the planning and execution of the D-Day invasion was exhibited for the first time yesterday at the Imperial War Museum — five years after it was commissioned.

It has taken that time for students of the Royal School of Needlework to complete the 264ft. long Overlord Embroidery, in 33 panels. Now the problem is where to put it—to exhibit it to best effect.

The chairman of the museum's trustees, Admiral Sir Deric Holland-Martin, said that plans to build a special gallery to house the embroidery would need a public contribution of about £70,000.

The trustees plan to build the gallery alongside the museum's west wing at a cost of £300,000, including £150,000 from the Government.

But these plans have not been approved by the Royal Fine Art Commission — and an alternative scheme could send the cost soaring.

The Overlord Tapestry — named after the code-name for the Normandy invasion — is 33ft. longer than the famous Bayeux Tapestry depicting the conquest of Britain by the Normans.

Express Newspapers/British Library

MEDIA INSPIRED

Donald Neilson had been considering the kidnap of Lesley Whittle for nearly three years – ever since he had read an article (above) in the *Daily Express* of 17 May 1972. The story gave details of the bequests left in the will of George Whittle, Lesley's father. Lesley had been left £82,500.

George Whittle, a one-time bus driver, had built up one of the most successful coach businesses in the Midlands, with a fleet of 70 vehicles.

In the same month that the Whittle story appeared, an article in the *Reader's Digest* gave an account of the kidnap in Atlanta, Georgia, of Barbara Mackle, an American student and heiress who was imprisoned in an underground cell. The kidnap, albeit unsuccessful, served as a model for Neilson.

A policeman (far left) wearing the clothes favoured by the Black Panther. He always wore white gloves, along with a dark boiler suit and black balaclava. Armed with a sawn-off shotgun and a dagger hanging from his belt, he sometimes carried a revolver too. Lesley was snatched in the early hours from the Whittle's house (left) in the Shropshire village of Highley. The kidnap message (above) was found later.

Far left: P.A.; left: S.I.; above: Express & Star, Wolverhampton

JAN-MARCH 1975

KEY DATES

14.1.75	Lesley Whittle is kidnapped from her bedroom
15.1.75	Gerald Smith shot at Dudley freight depot
16/17.1.75	Attempted delivery of ransom money
17.1.75	Death of Lesley Whittle
7.3.75	Discovery of Lesley Whittle's body

THE VICTIM

Popperfoto

STUDIOUS HEIRESS

Lesley Whittle's inheritance from her father was held in trust. Although the family lived in the largest house in the village of Highley, where the coach business was centred, Lesley did not live like a rich girl.

She was studying for her A-levels in pure and applied mathematics at a technical college in Wolverhampton, travelling there each day by public transport. She planned to go on to Sheffield University where her boyfriend was a student.

65 mile route to his hiding place.

Leaving the M6 at Junction 16, he drove to Bathpool Park. After removing a manhole cover leading into the central shaft of the drainage system, he returned to the car and released Lesley's legs.

Lesley's abductor forced her underground through an inspection hole just 11in wide, and then followed her down a rusty ladder. At its base was a 5ft step over which water flowed.

They reached the main shaft after a number of obstacles, including a waterfall, and finally arrived at the lowest of three platforms, just 24in wide and 62ft below ground. On the platform lay a foam rubber mattress, along with a sleeping bag. A wire noose, 5ft long, was already attached to the ladder.

Lesley was naked when her abductor placed the wire collar, which was cushioned with sticking plaster, around her neck. He clamped it on using three metal cable clips which he tightened with a spanner.

Lesley Whittle never discovered the identity of the man who kidnapped and entombed her in the Bathpool Park drainage system. In time, the public would know him as Donald Neilson.

The day after the kidnapping, Neilson forced Lesley to make two tape-recorded messages for her family, reading from what he had written in capital letters on a writing pad. The messages were to reassure them she was safe and urge them to pay the ransom money.

> **Her head was below the level of the platform. I saw her face, her eyes seemed to be half closed . . . I froze, then panicked**
>
> DONALD NEILSON

He also prepared a series of Dymo tape messages, which were to be used as part of the intricate plan to guide whoever had the ransom money to the pick-up point.

On the evening of 15 January, Neilson left Bathpool Park to make the final checks on the route that the ransom carrier was to follow and to conceal the Dymo tape messages in preselected telephone boxes.

Fatal challenge

While he was looking over the final pick-up point – a Freightliner depot near Dudley in Worcestershire – he was challenged by a night supervisor. Neilson shot the supervisor six times, mostly in the back, and escaped on foot, leaving his car behind. Inside the car were Lesley's slippers and the ransom messages she had recorded earlier that day.

On the following night, a second attempt was made to hand over the ransom money. Neilson changed the pick-up point to a wall adjoining Bathpool Park. After playing a new recording of instructions in Lesley's voice down the telephone, he waited for the ransom carrier.

The plan went disastrously wrong. Ronald Whittle, who was bringing the

Syndication International

Ronald Whittle (left), Lesley's older brother. He ran the coach firm bequeathed him by his father, and took phone messages from the kidnapper. Dorothy Whittle (below) was their mother.

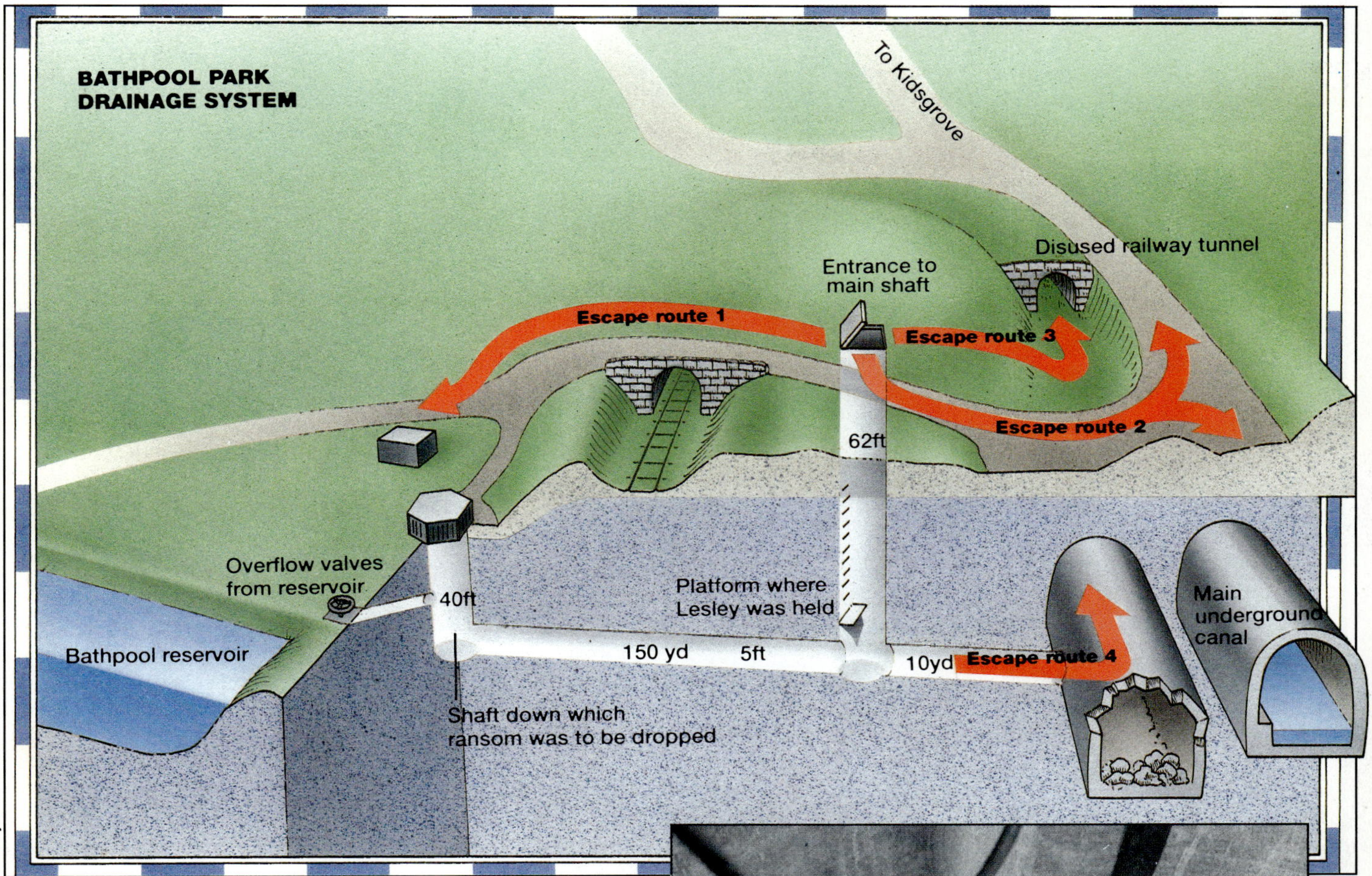

Chris Lyons

money, got lost and drove past the wall. A courting couple had parked in the exact spot where the handover was due to take place. Neilson became convinced that a police helicopter was hovering overhead and a trap was about to be sprung on him.

Act of panic?

Neilson returned to the underground platform where Lesley Whittle was noosed. According to his account, she moved over to give him space on the platform and fell over the edge. In the opinion of most others, including the jury at his trial, Neilson had panicked and pushed his hostage over the edge of the platform, where she died of shock or strangulation.

Lesley Whittle's body was found seven weeks later, still hanging from the length of wire coil in Bathpool Park. By this time the police were sure that the man they were looking for was also wanted in connection with the murders of three sub-post office masters in the past year. They had no clues as to his identity, but his individual style and ruthless operational methods had earned him a nickname with the police and general public – the Black Panther.

A cut-through map (above) shows Bathpool Park and its network of tunnels. Lesley Whittle was hidden in the central shaft. The ransom was to be dropped down the left-hand shaft and the Panther would collect it and escape along the dried out reservoir overflow tunnels that led to a disused canal tunnel. Alternative escape routes were planned overground or through an old railway tunnel. The main London to Manchester railway line ran through the Park. The photo (right) shows the shaft where Lesley was held captive.

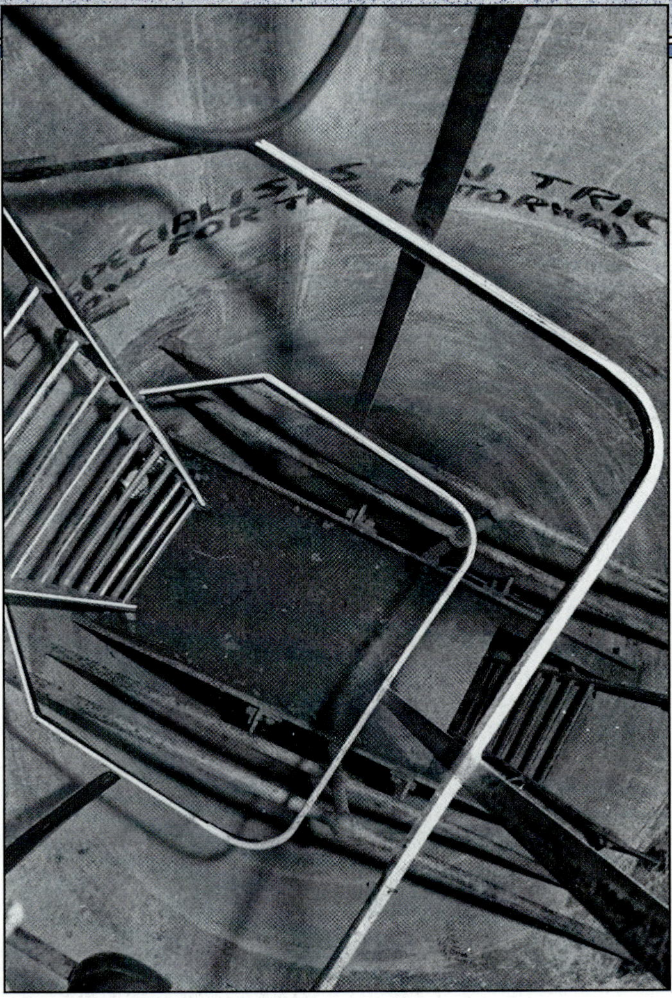

Express & Star, Wolverhampton

HOLDING A GRUDGE

Teased as a child, Neilson gained the self confidence from his army service to exact revenge on society.

Donald Neilson was born on 1 August 1936 in Morley, West Yorkshire, an extended suburb to the west of Leeds. He grew up in a cramped one up one down terraced house. His father was a poorly paid woollen worker and the family, like most other people in the neighbourhood, lived on the verge of poverty.

His real name was not Neilson but Nappey. This made him a natural target for bullies and teasing in his childhood. He was so affected by the experience that, when his own daughter was born, he decided to protect her from the same abuse by changing the family name to Neilson.

His mother died when he was ten years old. While his father carried on working, Neilson had to shoulder much of the responsibility of looking after his sister, who was four years younger.

Yorkshire Post

Neilson married Irene Tate in April 1955 (above). He was 18, she was 20. Two weeks later he joined his regiment (left) in Kenya.

By the time he was 17, he was working as an apprentice carpenter. He did not drink or smoke and his main pleasure seemed to be confined to going dancing in Bradford once a week.

It soon became clear that Neilson was a loner. None of his contemporaries can remember him having any more than one girlfriend – his future wife, Irene Tate, whom he met at a dance. Their secret wedding, to which even Irene's twin

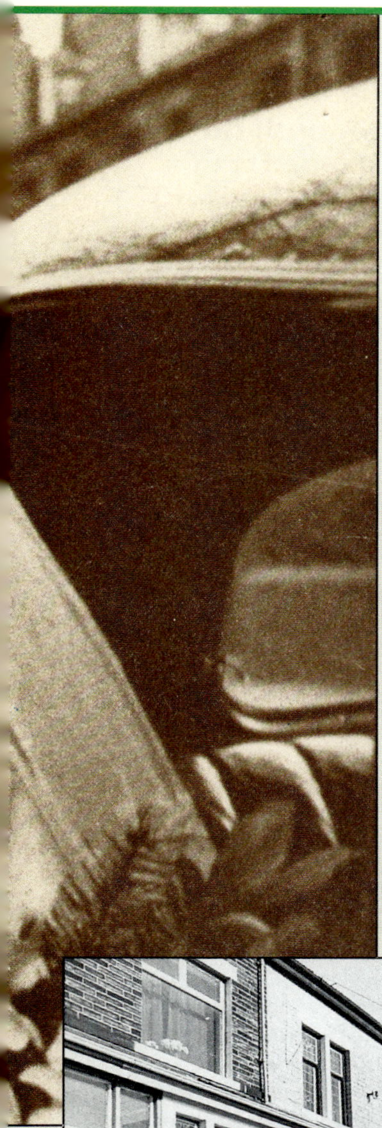

sister was not invited, took place in 1955.

Some time before that, Neilson had begun his National Service in the King's Own Yorkshire Light Infantry. He failed the initial ten week basic training course and had to be 'back-squadded' to repeat it. But his two years in the army had more of an influence on his later activities than anything else in his early life. He positively relished the hardships that military life forced on him.

Survival skills

Neilson spent six months in Kenya where he underwent an intensive period of jungle warfare training. He was equipped with a rubber-stocked, short-barrelled .303 jungle rifle, a weapon that bears a resemblance to a sawn-off shotgun.

Then after eight uneventful months in Aden, Neilson was posted to Cyprus. It was here that he was confronted most directly with death, when he had to guard terrorists awaiting execution.

On completion of his National Service, and having reached the rank of Lance Corporal, Neilson returned to West Yorkshire and his young wife. The army had instilled in him a sense of confidence and self-sufficiency. The young Neilson had played truant from school because he could not face the taunting. Now he was beginning to feel that he was in a position to exact revenge on society.

Donald and Irene Neilson bought a terraced home in Grangefield Avenue, alongside the busy Leeds Road leading out of Bradford. Despite the close-knit nature of the neighbourhood, the couple kept themselves to themselves and seldom invited anyone to their home. Their daughter Kathryn was born in 1960.

Most of the time Neilson made a living as a jobbing carpenter. He also tried to start up a small taxi business and at one stage planned to buy Alsatian guard dogs to start up a security firm. Despite all his efforts, however, financial success eluded him.

Military bearing

People remarked that Neilson walked with a parade ground spring in his step at all times and often gave the impression of taking orders at the double. He took to wearing paratrooper's boots, battledress jackets and olive green trousers. And he bought an ex-army jeep to drive around in.

KATHRYN NEILSON

By a bitter irony, there was less than six months' difference in age between Leslie Whittle and Neilson's only child, Kathryn. Apart from his dogs, she was the only known recipient of warmth and affection from Neilson. He attended her birth, fed and changed her when she was a baby, and made sure she could read and write before she started school.

As Kathryn grew into a pretty, dark-haired young woman, Neilson's grip over her and her mother seemed to tighten. She was rarely allowed out of the house, unless it was to take one of the dogs for a walk with her mother, or to go swimming with him as part of his fitness regime. His overbearing attitude began to put a strain on the relationship with his wife and daughter.

Syndication International; inset: Express & Star, Wolverhampton

The house with the 'sale' sign (above) was home to Donald and Irene Neilson and their daughter Kathryn for 15 years. It is in Grangefield Avenue, Thornaby, Bradford. In a locked attic room, police found a great deal of evidence that linked Neilson to the murders. The copy of Neilson's birth certificate (right) shows the surname that gave Donald such torment.

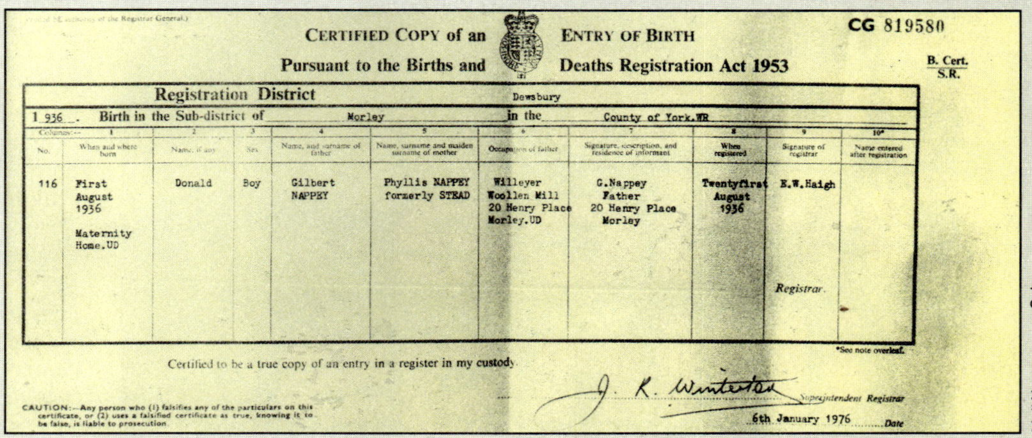

(Printed by authority of the Registrar General.)

CG 819580

CERTIFIED COPY of an ENTRY OF BIRTH

Pursuant to the Births and Deaths Registration Act 1953

B. Cert. S.R.

Registration District Dewsbury

1936. Birth in the Sub-district of Morley in the County of York.WR

No.	When and where born	Name, if any	Sex	Name, and surname of father	Name, surname and maiden surname of mother	Occupation of father	Signature, description, and residence of informant	When registered	Signature of registrar	Name entered after registration
Columns:—	1	2	3	4	5	6	7	8	9	10*
116	First August 1936 Maternity Home.UD	Donald	Boy	Gilbert NAPPEY	Phyllis NAPPEY formerly STEAD	Willeyer Woollen Mill 20 Henry Place Morley.UD	G.Nappey Father 20 Henry Place Morley	Twentyfirst August 1936	E.W.Haigh Registrar.	

*See note overleaf.

Certified to be a true copy of an entry in a register in my custody.

J. R. Winterton Superintendent Registrar

6th January 1976 Date

CAUTION:—Any person who (1) falsifies any of the particulars on this certificate, or (2) uses a falsified certificate as true, knowing it to be false, is liable to prosecution.

Mail Newspapers-Solo

TWO

THE MURDER

The Post Office Killings

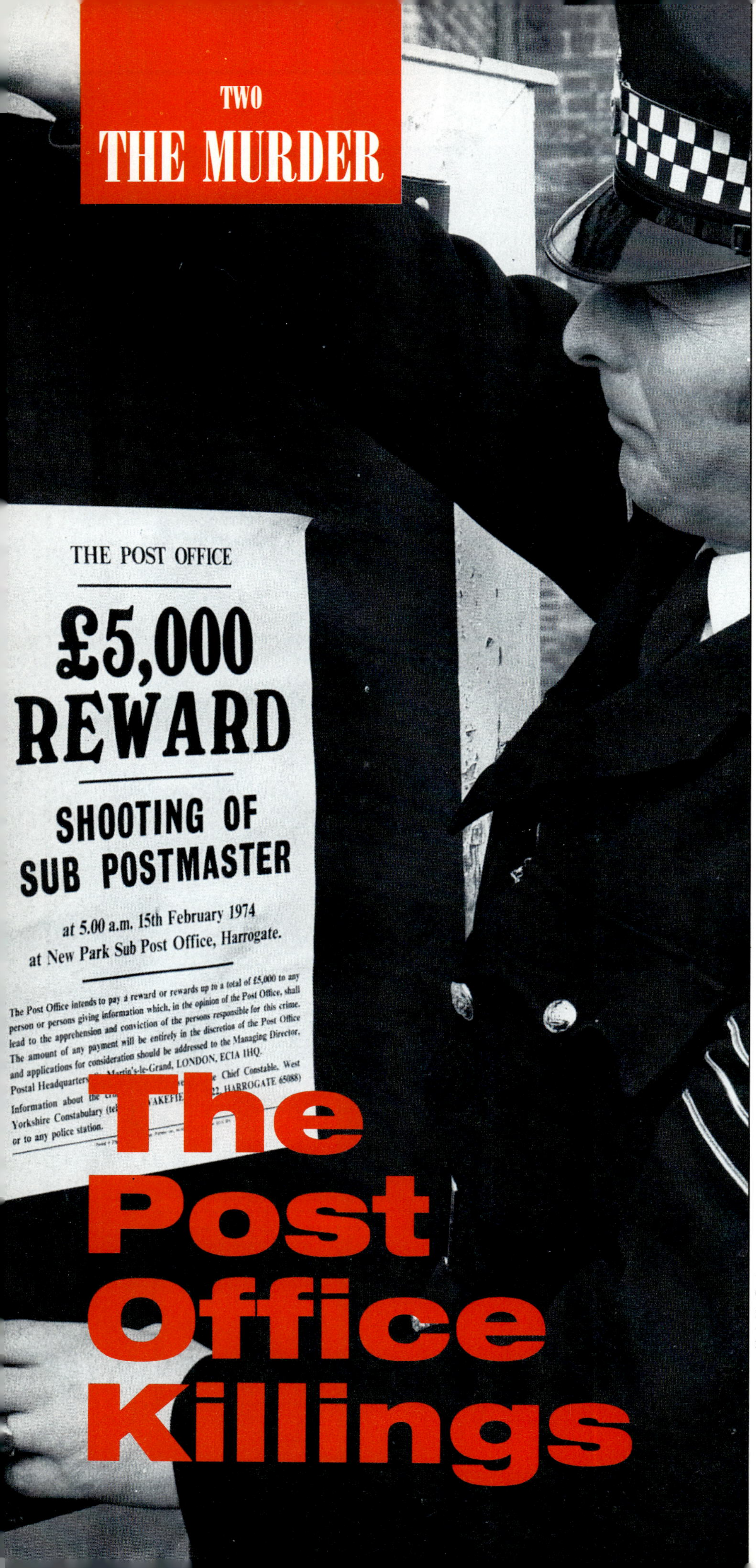

Yorkshire Post

It was not until the vicious shotgun murder of a sub-postmaster in 1974 that police realized they were hunting a psychopath – a hooded killer whose territory of violence would soon stretch from north to south.

Some time in 1965, Donald Neilson turned to house-breaking in order to supplement his income. Using a manual brace and bit drill, he developed a technique of making holes in window frames through which he could manipulate the catch with a piece of strong wire or a fine screwdriver.

The burglaries became very familiar to the Yorkshire police and became known as the 'brace and bit' robberies. By the time Neilson was arrested in 1975, over 400 such robberies had been committed, all of which the police felt they could close files on.

No return

The returns on these burglaries were small, however, and Neilson remained dissatisfied. He was a loner who disliked authority and was jealous of those who were wealthier than he was.

Like every other money-making venture Neilson had attempted, the burglaries did not bring in enough to change his way of life. He may have proved to be extremely proficient at getting in and out of people's homes as they slept, but he rarely seemed able to choose where much money was to be found.

In 1967 Neilson expanded his range of criminal activities when he raided a sub-post office in Nottingham. It was the first of 19 similar raids, almost exclusively in Lancashire and Yorkshire, between 1967 and 1974.

The advantages of choosing sub-post offices as a target was that the security arrangements were fare less rigorous than at a main branch or local bank. In the early 1970s there were more than 23,000 sub-post offices in Britain, providing a

The Post Office offered £5,000 reward for information about the Panther after the murder of Donald Skepper. By the end of the year it had reached £25,000.

Yorkshire Post

The Black Panther broke into Donald Skepper's sub-post office (above) in the early hours of 15 February 1974, by releasing the security catch on the rear window.

seemingly limitless number of potential places to raid. The disadvantage was simply that the amount of money to be taken from each one was small. No one could retire from a life of crime after raiding a sub-post office.

Since his National Service in the army, Neilson had remained obsessed with military organization and planning. To carry out his night visits he had established a headquarters at his home in Grangefield Avenue. Half of the lounge was a workshop, equipped with the tools of his trade, while the other half was boarded off to serve as an office. He would sit in his office dreaming of future operations that would make him and his family wealthy.

> **I was holding the shotgun with both hands. As the man came forward and grabbed the shotgun I pulled away to escape. The gun went off**
>
> DONALD NEILSON on the murder of Donald Skepper

To the outside world, the Neilson family were private to the point of being reclusive. When Donald Neilson was seen, he was working compulsively – either mending one of his vehicles or repainting the house. Mrs Neilson was hardly ever seen outside the house, and neighbours noted how poorly dressed she was when she did appear.

On 16 February 1972, Neilson broke into a sub-post office in Haywood, Lancashire. The postmaster, Leslie Richardson, was woken up and, getting out of bed, found himself confronted by a hooded man who spoke to him in what sounded like a West Indian accent. In the struggle that followed, Neilson's shotgun went

THE VICTIMS

Donald Skepper, 50, was shot as he was about to tackle Neilson. He died shortly after.

Derek Astin, 43, was gunned down after he awoke and confronted the Panther. He died in hospital.

Press Association

Sidney Grayland, 55, was killed by a single shot from the Panther's .22 rifle after a short struggle.

KEY DATES

FEB 72-NOV 74

16.2.72	Leslie Richardson injured in raid on Heywood sub-post office
May 1972	*Daily Express* runs Whittle story
15.2.74	Donald Skepper killed in Harrogate
6.9.74	Derek Astin killed in Higher Baxenden
11.11.74	Sidney Grayland killed in Langley

£5,000 REWARD OFFERED FOR KILLER OF POSTMASTER

Mr Derek Astin.

By JAMES O'BRIEN

A SUB-POSTMASTER convalescing in bandages after an operation, was shot and killed by a hooded gunman yesterday. His arm was almost shot off as his wife tried to beat off the killer with a vacuum cleaner.

The Post Office has offered a £5,000 reward for information leading to the arrest of the killer of Mr Derek Astin, 43, at Accrington, Lancs.

Press coverage of the killings was fairly low-key and did not provide the scale of publicity the police required. Only when Lesley Whittle was abducted did the Panther become major news.

BACKGROUND

FAMILY WAR GAMES

When police broke into Neilson's attic they found a macabre collection of weapons and quasi-military clothing. They also uncovered a family photograph album. Instead of happy family scenes, photographs showed the Neilsons, dressed up as soldiers, 'playing' at war.

One showed Neilson playing the part of a dead 'enemy', hanging from the wreckage of a still-burning jeep. Another was of Kathryn pulling a sheet over the supposedly dead body of her mother. A third showed 'commander' Neilson, pointing to a map in the 'jungle' clearing.

During these mock manoeuvres, Neilson would make bazookas and mortars with pieces of drain pipe, and German-type hand-grenades from Coca-Cola tins. Neilson's daughter, Kathryn, told how he would force the family to spend weeks in military-style encampments, with a camouflage net spread over the trees, only a quarter of a mile from their home.

off, blowing a hole in the ceiling. Mr Richardson managed to snatch off the hood and was surprised to see a white man since he used a West Indian accent.

Neilson escaped through a rear door. The police afterwards felt sure that the raid was linked with seven similar break-ins and for the first time had a witness who could put together a Photofit identification of the raider. It was to be the first of six such Photofits, none of which produced a realistic likeness.

Almost exactly two years later, Donald Neilson was in Harrogate, Yorkshire. His target was a sub-post office corner shop run by Donald and Johanna Skepper. The couple had lived and worked there for ten years and on the night of 15 February, they were asleep upstairs, with their 18 year-old son Richard in the adjoining bedroom.

Bound and gagged

Neilson drilled three holes in a rear, ground-floor casement window to gain access, and then moved silently upstairs to the son's bedroom. Richard was shaken awake to find Neilson standing in front of him pointing a shotgun at his face and wearing a black mask.

Neilson demanded to know where the safe keys were kept. After being told they were in a cupboard at the bottom of the stairs he pressed a piece of tape over the boy's mouth, bound his wrists together and taped his ankles to the bed.

Neilson could not find the keys and returned to the son's bedroom. He released him and forced him in to his parents' bedroom to find the keys. As Richard Skepper moved past the foot of the bed his mother and father woke up, instinctively reaching for the bedside light to see who was in the room.

Fatal decision

Neilson stepped quickly inside the bedroom and ordered Skepper to switch the light off again. In that split-second, Skepper made the brave but fateful decision that was to cost him his life. Jumping out of bed, he shouted to his son 'Let's get him.' Neilson, who was standing just two feet away from the sub-post master, responded by shooting him in the chest. Donald Skepper fell dying into his wife's arms.

'It was horrifying,' she said later. 'If it was someone you could have seen the face of, or someone you could have spoken to reasonably . . . but just to see the hood was really terrifying, so much so that I really couldn't move.'

Neilson rushed from the room, with his shotgun in one hand and a wooden-handled knife with a four-inch blade in the other. It was 5.25 a.m. when Richard Skepper raised the alarm. 'My mother woke up first and then my father sat up in bed,' he said later. 'The intruder came into the room carrying his gun in his right hand. He was not pointing it at anyone in particular, just generally around the room. My father said something like "What do you want?" to the intruder, and I said he wanted the keys. My father made as if to get out of bed, swinging his legs around to face the man. He said, "Let's get him." At that point the man who was holding the gun pointed it at my father. The next thing I saw was a

> **"I did all these things, but I must tell you the truth of what happened. I want to make statements about them all"**
>
> DONALD NEILSON

THE MURDER TRAIL

Donald Neilson had been raiding post offices and burgling houses for two years before he committed his first murder. Following his arrest, police in the North closed the files on more than 400 unsolved house-breaking offences, many of which, in Yorkshire at least, were known as the 'brace and bit' robberies. He was also responsible for 16 other sub-post office robberies, all committed between 1967 and 1973.

By the time of the first murder at the beginning of 1972, police already had a Photofit picture of the man who would become Public Enemy No. 1. Two years earlier sub-postmaster Leslie Richardson had snatched off Neilson's black hood during an attempted robbery.

By the end of 1974, the 'heat' generated by a string of robberies and two murders was such that Neilson travelled south, away from Yorkshire and Lancashire.

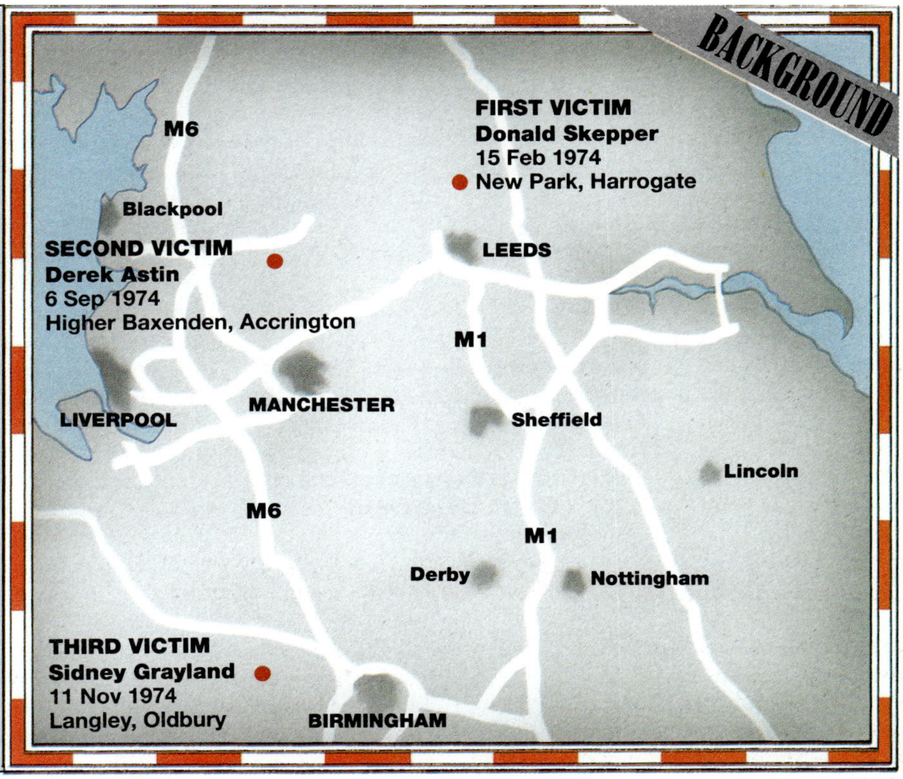

Chris Lyons

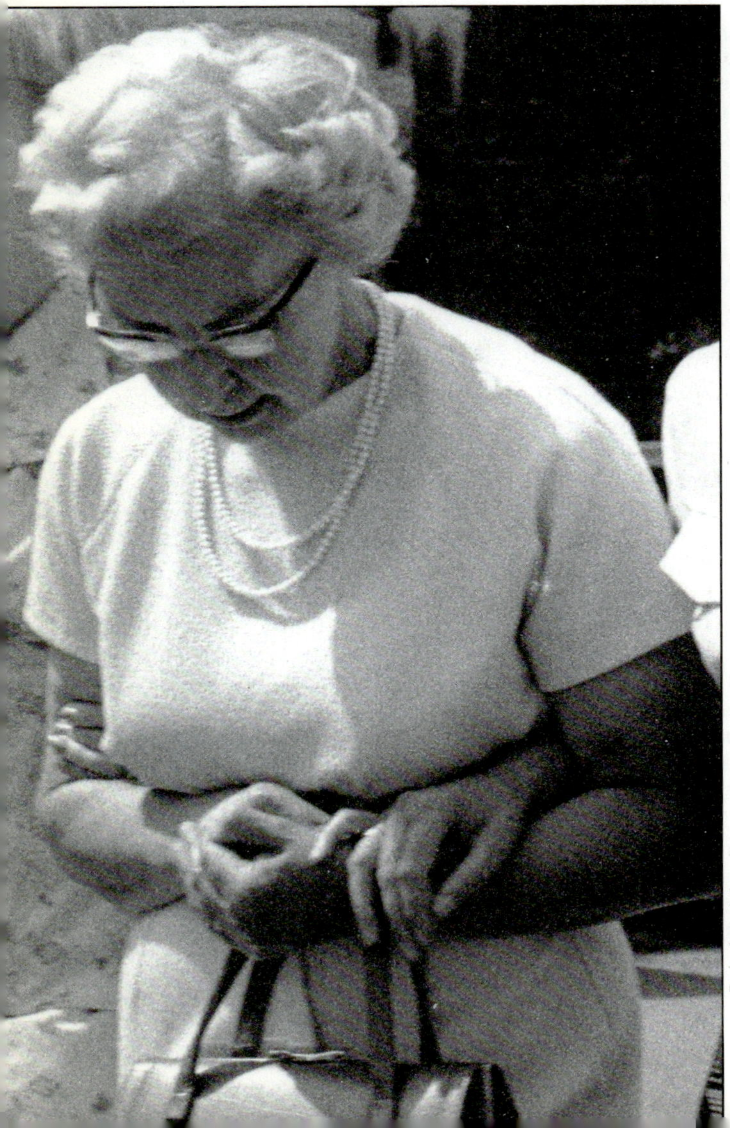

Press Association

Margaret Grayland (left) leaves court after giving a tearful account of the night she found her husband, Sidney, dying from a gunshot wound. Mrs Grayland was savagely beaten after seeing the Panther's face. Her next recollection was waking up in hospital days later, only to be told that her husband was dead. The police acquired major evidence after the murder – the blood-soaked cord used to bind Margaret Grayland, six unused .22 bullets, five spent cartridges and a piece of the finger of a rubber glove that Neilson had been wearing.

flash of the gun going off and then I heard the explosion. My father fell back on to the bed.'

The police surrounded Harrogate with armed officers, but Neilson had got away. Within a few days, more than a thousand people had been interviewed and the Post Office had offered a £5,000 reward. The police had no idea that Neilson lived less than half-an-hour's drive away.

> **My God, this was a bad one. You might as well know it was me**
>
> DONALD NEILSON on the murder of Sidney Grayland

By the following September, seven months later, 30,000 people had been interviewed, but the police were no closer to identifying the Black Panther. In the early hours of 6 September, Neilson re-emerged to kill again.

It was after 4 a.m. when Mr Derek Astin woke up in his flat above the sub-post office in the village of Higher Baxendin, near Accrington, in Lancashire. He lived there with his wife Marion and their two children, 13 year-old Susan and 10 year-old Stephen. When Mrs Astin woke up she found her husband was already out of bed and grappling with a hooded figure by the wardrobe.

Mr Astin pushed Neilson on to the landing and his wife, searching desperately for a weapon, tried to hand him a vacuum cleaner. There was then a loud 'crack', and Mr Astin collapsed on the landing. At the same time, Neilson fell backwards down the narrow, steep staircase. In the midst of her terror, Mrs Astin noticed how quickly he recovered and got up again.

Mr Astin suffered a massive wound which severed both the main artery and the main vein in his arm. His daughter tried to use a bedsheet to staunch the flow of blood, before rushing out of the house to find help. Their telephone wires had been cut, and Astin died soon after arriving at the hospital.

There were already 100 policemen trying to solve the Skepper murder, and when detectives arrived in Accrington, there was no doubt that the double killer was the same person who had been unmasked by Leslie Richardson two years earlier in Lancashire.

> **We always said that if anyone broke in, our life was more precious than the money – but we were not even given that chance**
>
> MRS SIDNEY GRAYLAND

First of all there was the telltale brace and bit method of entry in all three incidents. There was also the bullet taken from Astin, and a spent cartridge case, which were added to the collection of linked ballistic evidence. The police had already received further confirmation that they were dealing with a man who was ruthlessly callous. However, while the officers heading the inquiry realized they were dealing with an extremely dangerous man, the public at large remained ignorant of the fact.

Even when 55 year-old Sidney Grayland was shot and killed just nine weeks later at the sub-post office run by his wife, Margaret, at Langley in the West Midlands, the national press was still treating the shootings as isolated crimes.

Unhooded

The Graylands were stock-taking in the early evening of 11 November, when Sidney Grayland went out to the storeroom. His wife heard a shot and when she rushed to investigate, found her husband on the floor, wounded in the stomach. Neilson had entered through the back door with a bottle of ammonia strapped to the torch he was carrying. When he knocked on the door and Mr Grayland opened it, the older man was also carrying a torch. In the struggle that followed, Mr Grayland grabbed the intruder's hand and the ammonia squirted into Neilson's hooded face.

Temporarily blinded, Neilson ripped the hood from his head, lashing out with his foot at the same time. At that moment Mrs Grayland arrived and was told by her husband, 'Watch it, Peg, I have been hit.' Neilson realized that Mrs Grayland must have seen his face. He attacked her, fracturing her skull in three places. He left her in a pool of blood, covering her head and shoulders with cardboard boxes.

Before leaving, Neilson removed cash and postal orders totalling £800. It was to be more than four hours before the events at the Graylands' shop were discovered. At 10.55 p.m., two policemen noticed that the lights were still on at the shop. When they investigated they found Mr Grayland dead and his wife barely clinging to life.

The police now had more clues, including another .22 bullet, five spent cartridges and a length of blood-soaked cord that Neilson had used to bind Mrs Grayland's wrists.

Express & Star, Wolverhampton

IN CONTEXT

IRENE NEILSON

Donald Neilson married 20 year-old Irene Tate at St Paul's Church, Morley, on 30 April 1955. Neilson, or Nappey, as he was still known, was only 18 and doing National Service. He had met Irene at a dance hall in Bradford. There were no guests at the wedding, and the bride's family were uneasy about the marriage.

The newlyweds regularly let themselves into Irene's mother's house in Bradford, when she was out, which she was unhappy about.

Hilda Tate, Irene's twin sister, noticed a gradual change in Irene's attitude and behaviour after the marriage. Irene became very withdrawn and would ask Hilda to leave by the back door if she heard Neilson arriving home. When Neilson was present, he would virtually ignore Hilda.

£25,000 REWARD

Shooting of three Sub-postmasters:—

1. **About 5 a.m. on Friday, 15th February, 1974, at New Park Sub Post Office, Harrogate, Yorks.**
2. **About 4 a.m. on Friday, 6th September, 1974, at Higher Baxenden Sub Post Office, Accrington, Lancs.**
3. **On the evening of 11th November, 1974, at Langley Sub Post Office, Oldbury, Birmingham.**

The Post Office and the National Federation of Sub-postmasters intend, jointly, to pay a reward or rewards up to a total of **£25,000** to any person or persons giving information which, in the opinion of the Post Office, shall lead to the apprehension and conviction of the person or persons responsible for all or **any** of these crimes.

The Murdered Sub-Postmasters

DONALD SKEPPER
Harrogate

DEREK ASTIN
Accrington

SIDNEY GRAYLAND
Oldbury

Express Newspapers

Police stand guard outside Langley sub-post office (above), the day after the murder of Sidney Grayland. The crime was discovered by two constables, Roger Toghill and Philip Rich, at 10.55 p.m., four hours after the attack. Neilson got away with postal orders and £800 cash. The brutality of the attack prompted the Post Office to increase the reward (right).

Mrs Grayland herself was unconscious for some time after the attack and even when she had begun to recover, could not provide a description of her attacker. At this stage, detectives were unwilling to make an official link between the Grayland murder and the previous two post office attacks.

They were also unaware that the man they were looking for was about to embark on a far more ambitious scheme. After two years of planning and physical training, Donald Neilson was ready to try kidnapping a victim for ransom.

It was only the second time such a thing had been tried in Britain. And though the first attempt had ended in failure, Donald Neilson believed that his military precision would make it pay off.

THE BLACK PANTHER'S LAIR

Press Association

Within minutes of Neilson revealing his identity to police, murder squad detectives swooped on his house in Bradford. They found a chilling collection of Rambo-style equipment.

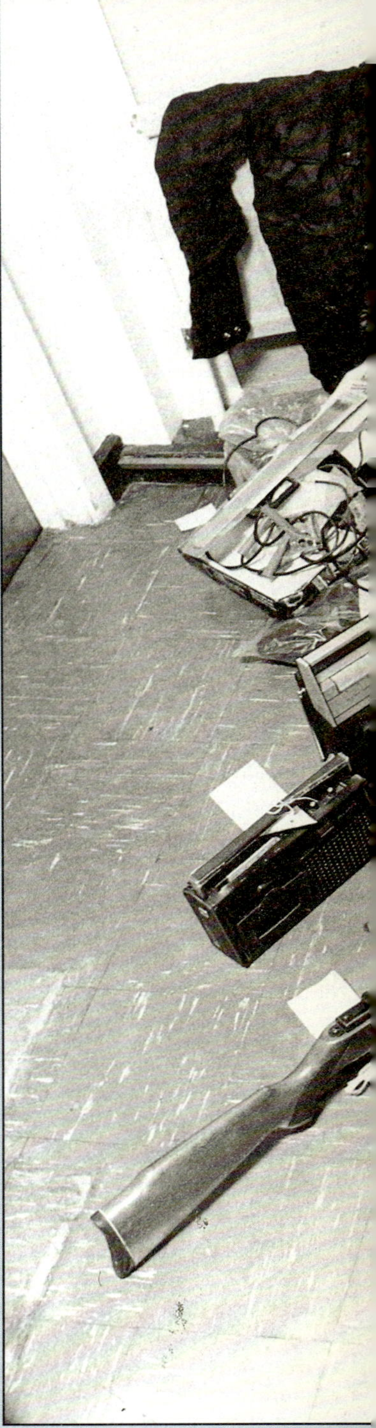

Syndication International

Yorkshire Post

In the attic (left) of Neilson's house in Grangefield Avenue (top, left), police found a bizarre assortment of murder weapons and clothing. As well as dozens of anoraks and jackets, detectives also found balls of string, sub-aqua equipment, ropes, haversacks, radios, over 700 car ignition keys, a wig and assorted equipment, including a Polar suit and knives.

Hidden inside the roof void of Neilson's attic were a sawn-off Remington shotgun, fitted with a home-made silencer, and more than 1,000 rounds of ammunition. The macabre murder kit (right and above) also included a .22 rifle with a telescopic sight and a number of spent .22 cartridges. Police also found hoods and coils of wire similar to that used to hang Lesley Whittle.

Press Association

THREE

THE HUNT

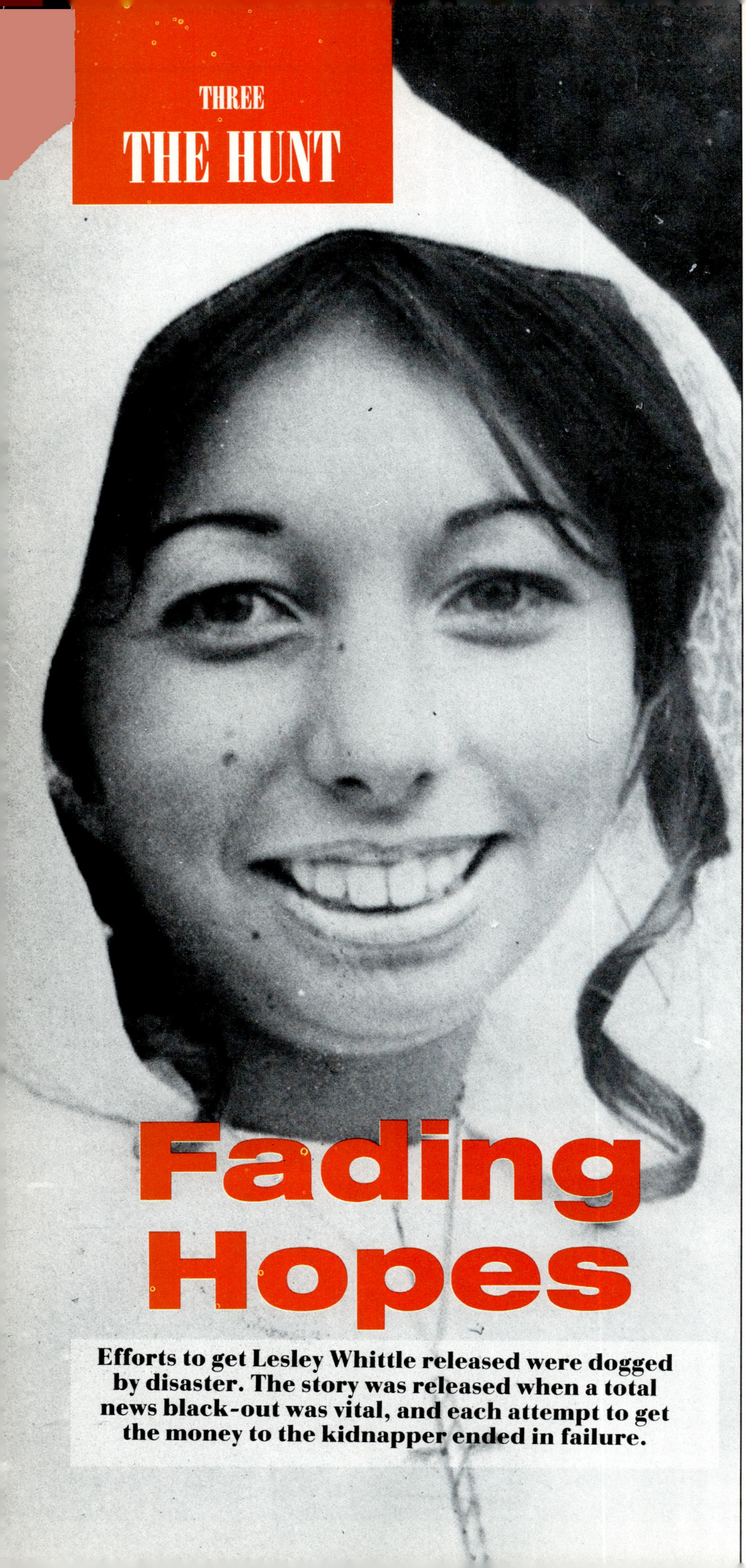

Fading Hopes

Efforts to get Lesley Whittle released were dogged by disaster. The story was released when a total news black-out was vital, and each attempt to get the money to the kidnapper ended in failure.

Dorothy Whittle woke on the morning of 14 January 1975, to discover that her daugher Lesley was missing. She was puzzled – in the early hours of the morning Lesley had been fast asleep in her room. After checking the house to make certain her daughter was not there, Mrs Whittle drove the length of Highley's main street to her son Ronald's house in the vain hope that Lesley had spent the night there.

Neither Ronald nor his wife, Gaynor, had seen or heard from Lesley that morning.

In deep unease, Mrs Whittle and Gaynor drove back to the Whittles' home. There they discovered the ransom demands and realized they were in the midst of a full-blown nightmare – Lesley had been kidnapped.

Ransom demands

There were three ransom messages, all on a coil of Dymo tape left on a box resting on a flower vase in the lounge. The messages read:

- No police £50,000 ransom to be ready to deliver wait for telephone call at Swan shopping centre telephone box 6 p.m. to 1 p.m. if no call return following evening when you answer call give your name only and listen you must follow instructions without argument from the time you answer you are on a time limit if police or tricks death.
- Swan shopping centre Kidderminster deliver £50,000 in a white suitcase.

Left: Syndication International; right: Express & Star, Wolverhampton

• £50,000 all in old notes £25,000 in £1 notes and £25,000 in £5 there will be no exchange only after £50,000 has been cleared will victim be released.

Detective Chief Superintendent Bob Booth, head of West Mercia CID, was investigating a murder in Wellington, Shropshire, when he heard the news from Highley.

> **If you plan for bloodhounds, you will beat the police alsatians**
> DONALD NEILSON

When he heard about the professionally prepared ransom tapes and the cut telephone wires, he went straight to the Whittle home.

Ronald Whittle immediately set about raising the £50,000 in used notes from his bank in Bridgnorth. At this stage, the police were not certain the kidnap was genuine, but they arranged to tap the Whittles' telephone and a telephone box at Kidderminster that Neilson had referred to in his ransom note. They also set up a tail for Ronald Whittle and informed Scotland Yard.

Like the American FBI, who had a kidnap conviction rate of 240 out of 400 in the previous four years, Superintendent Booth encouraged the family to co-operate fully with the kidnapper. He was willing for them to pay the ransom if it secured the early release of the victim on the grounds that the majority of kidnap victims do not survive more than the first 48 hours.

Booth also accepted Scotland Yard's offer of 12 experts who had been trained in techniques to deal with cases of kidnapping. Despite the acrimony that was to develop over the weeks between West Mercia CID and Scotland Yard, during the first few hours they agreed on one thing. Ronald Whittle should take the ransom money and wait in the telephone box in Kidderminster from 6 p.m. onwards for the next instructions.

But by 8 p.m., there had been a development that was to influence the entire investigation. It was crucial that the kidnapper be given no hint that the Whittle family had involved the police. Yet somehow a freelance reporter received a tip-off that a major kidnap incident was underway.

As a result, the police took the decision to withdraw Ronald Whittle from the telephone box in Kidderminster just before 9.30 p.m. When Neilson finally telephoned just before midnight, the police tapper could hear the call ringing in, but there was nobody in the box to answer it.

A newspaper poster provides the face, the name and the emergency telephone number. But no one had seen Lesley Whittle.

Express & Star, Wolverhampton

On 14 February 1975, just over a month after the kidnapping, police converged on acres of scrubland at Gornal Wood (left), a mile from the centre of Sedgley. Thirty seven dogs were used in the search, as over 100 police officers used sticks to turn over the foliage. The hunt followed a tip from a woman who saw a car on the waste ground three days before. Nothing was found.

TAPED MESSAGE

IN CONTEXT

A tape-recording of Lesley Whittle's voice was among the incriminating items found in the stolen car following Neilson's shooting of Gerald Smith. When Neilson forced her to make the tape, Lesley had been 60ft underground, naked and bound hand and foot. The tape began, 'Please mum,' and contained directions to a phone box, where further instructions would be found.

Superintendent Bob Booth took the decision to broadcast the tape. While it would cause distress to family and friends, he hoped that the sound of Lesley's voice would prick the conscience of anyone harbouring the kidnapper. The tape was broadcast on Midland Television, but the huge response led nowhere.

When the tape was played during his trial, Neilson wept to hear Lesley's plaintive voice reassuring her mother: 'There's no need to worry mum. I'm OK. I got a bit wet but I'm quite dry now. I'm being treated very well. OK?'

KEY DATES

JAN-MARCH 75

14.1.75	Lesley Whittle's disappearance discovered
14.1.75	Story leaked to press
15.1.75	Gerald Smith shot
16.1.75	Final ransom delivery attempt fails
23.1.75	Stolen Morris 1300 discovered in Dudley Freightliner depot
5.3.75	Ronald Whittle and Inspector Booth in confrontation

The following night, 15 January, police again instructed Ronald Whittle to leave the telephone box during the time that Neilson had arranged to ring. The reason this time was a hoax caller who had managed to convince them his call was genuine. As a result, Ronald wasted a night driving to a non-existent delivery destination.

On the same night, while Neilson was preparing the second part of his plan to secure the ransom money, he shot Gerald Smith, a security guard, at the Freightliner depot in Dudley.

Misleading information

Gerald Smith survived for 14 months after the attack, with the help of four operations. He provided the police with what he was convinced was a good likeness of the Black Panther. His attacker had spoken with a local accent, from the village of Tipton less than two miles from Dudley. This well-intentioned evidence proved extremely misleading.

ILLEGAL MURDER

Gerald Smith, shot by Neilson, died 14 months later, a time lapse that meant Neilson could not be charged with murder. Following an assault, if the victim does not die within a year and a day, death is legally attributed to some other cause – an 'irrebuttable presumption'. So Neilson was charged with the *attempted* murder of Smith.

The law was tested in the Dyson case of 13 November 1906. Dyson attacked his baby son and was sent to prison for assault. The baby died 5 March 1908 and Dyson was convicted of murder. But the Court of Appeal quashed the conviction.

BACKGROUND

Yorkshire Post

> **I used to bath and go out in clean clothes, possibly disinfected, in order that there would be no scent for the dogs to follow**
>
> DONALD NEILSON

In his hurry to escape from the depot, Neilson left his stolen car, a green Morris 1300, in a car park just 150 yards from where Gerald Smith had been shot. For eight days it remained unnoticed. As a result, the kidnapping of Lesley Whittle and the shooting in Dudley became two separate news stories.

Finally a policeman noticed that the car's registration number on the road tax did not match the number plates. Further investigation revealed that the car had been stolen from West Bromwich over three months before.

When the Morris was searched, the boot revealed some startling clues. There was a tape-recording of Lesley Whittle's voice, which was intended for the abortive ransom collection of 15 January. Also inside were tape recorders, torches, a gun and ammunition and a foam mattress. The gun provided the first positive link between the sub-post office murders and the Whittle kidnap.

On the third night of the kidnap, 16 January, the police felt sure they would get the money to the kidnapper. The Scotland Yard officers had brought sophisticated bugging and surveillance equipment. Several of them were armed. A special squad of vehicles was on stand-by and a mobile headquarters was ready to coordinate the investigation.

New instructions

The kidnapper called at 11.45 p.m. Leonard Rudd, the transport manager of Whittle's Coaches, answered the call. Lesley's recorded voice instructed the ransom carrier to wait by the Kidsgrove telephone box.

Ronald Whittle drove first to Bridgnorth police station where he was briefed by Detective Chief Superintendent Lovejoy of Scotland Yard,

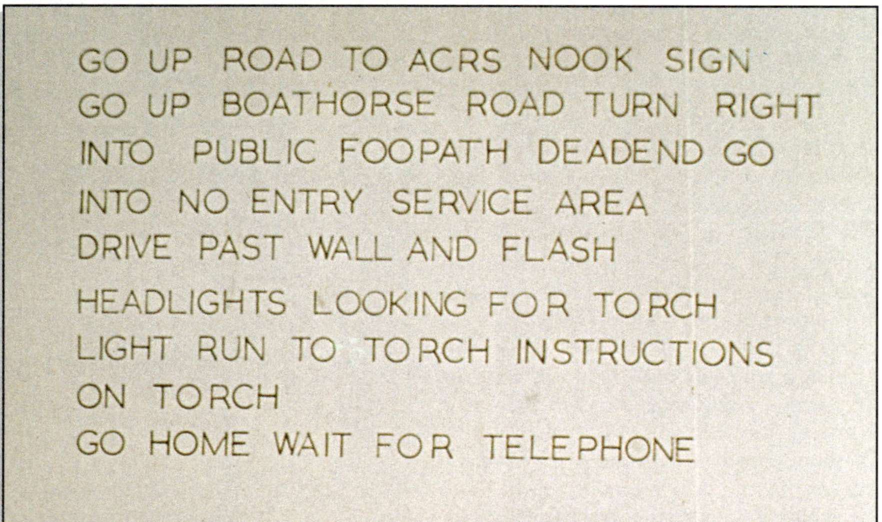

Metropolitan Police

Ronald Whittle found these instructions (left) in Dymo tape at a telephone booth in Kidsgrove during the third and last attempt to pay the ransom. The plan went tragically awry.

who was in charge of this part of the operation. Without Booth's knowledge, the Scotland Yard officers had also decided to record on microfilm the serial number of every bank note.

Ronald Whittle set off to deliver the ransom money at almost 1.30 a.m. His uncertainty was compounded by the fact that there was nothing but the kidnapper's word to assure him that his own life was not in danger. The Panther could shoot him and escape with the money. And there was also the chilling possibility that Lesley was already dead.

Frustrating journey

Unmarked police cars kept a discreet distance from Ronald Whittle's car. A total of 11 other surveillance vehicles were involved in the operation. Yet Whittle twice lost his way and it was 3 a.m. before he reached the first contact point. It took him a further 30 minutes to locate the hidden message.

From Kidsgrove, Ronald Whittle was instructed to go to Bathpool Park, where he was to go to a wall and wait for a flashing light signal. Once at Bathpool Park, Ronald waited with mounting frustration for the signal. It never came. Finally and reluctantly,

Police display the stolen Morris car (below) and equipment (right), found after the shooting of Gerald Smith. Neilson chose common brands which would not attract attention. But his survival kit indicated an unusual man, used to living rough in harsh conditions.

Express & Star, Wolverhampton; inset: Syndication International

Chief Superintendent Bob Booth (left, centre) and a senior colleague play a tape by the kidnapped Lesley Whittle in a final bid to jog people's memories.

Express & Star, Wolverhampton

he pulled out after lengthy consultations with the police over two radios in his car.

Whittle could not have known that Neilson had worked out in advance how long the journey should have taken. Nor did he realize that a courting couple had driven into the park at 2.30 a.m., at least an hour before he arrived, and were puzzled to see a torch flashing in their direction. The couple said later they also saw a police car inside the park, a claim fiercely denied by the police.

Wrong conclusion

Neilson had been watching all these activities through a pair of field glasses. Convinced that police were about to move in on him and that the ransom would never be paid, Neilson fell into a rage, returned to the drainage shaft and murdered Lesley Whittle. By dawn, he was on his way back to Bradford.

When daylight arrived the Scotland Yard team searched Bathpool Park as discreetly as possible. They assumed that Neilson might still be inside the park and were keen to give the impression that Ronald Whittle had gone there without their knowledge. They found none of the clues that could have led them to the underground hideout.

Local suspicions

The hunt for the identity of Lesley Whittle's kidnapper had by now centred around the family's home village of Highley. Detectives believed that anyone with a knowledge of Lesley's financial circumstances, and where she lived, was very likely to be a local. Moreover, the kidnapper seemed to have an intimate knowledge of the Whittle home. While an RAF helicopter hovered over the village looking for possible hideouts, detectives interviewed anyone who could possibly be a suspect.

Other theories circulated. One was the possibility that the kidnapper was a travelling salesman who had become familiar with Highley. Another was that he had worked at Dudley Zoo,

BACKGROUND

BOB BOOTH

Detective Chief Superintendent Bob Booth, who as head of the West Mercia CID led the hunt for Neilson, was an exceptionally gifted detective. But the Black Panther case, and particularly the Lesley Whittle kidnap, left him bitterly disillusioned.

He believed he was left to take responsibility for other people's actions. In particular he blamed Staffordshire Police for the appearance of a panda car at the ransom rendezvous site, which probably frightened Neilson off at a crucial moment. Lesley Whittle died minutes later. Staffordshire Police strongly denied the patrol car was one of theirs.

Booth also criticized Scotland Yard officers for delaying Ronald Whittle at Bridgnorth Police Station when they briefed him for the ransom drop. The officers had insisted on recording every banknote on microfilm.

Syndication International

which was situated next to the Freightliner depot where Gerald Smith was shot.

The police were prepared to clutch at such straws because they knew they were working against the clock.

Confrontation

Chief Superintendent Booth knew that the most important clues were still likely to lie within the grounds of Bathpool Park. But he was unwilling to move in until he felt certain that the chances of finding Lesley alive there were minimal. On the evening of 5 March, Booth and Ronald Whittle appeared on television and acted out a pre-arranged confrontation with each other.

Ronald Whittle pretended to reveal for the first time to Booth that he had gone to Bathpool Park and attempted to deliver the ransom money. Booth's response was to fly into a rage and terminate the interview. To the viewing public it appeared that Booth had been humiliated. For Bob Booth, however, this deception provided the opportunity to find out what was in Bathpool Park.

Bathpool Park (below), the scene of the Panther's most notorious crime. Neilson came to be familiar with every inch of the landscape, but failed to make his handover instructions clear to Ronald Whittle.

RONALD WHITTLE'S CRUEL ORDEAL

For Ronald Whittle, the ordeal of his sister's kidnap was made worse by the suspicions that fell on himself. Though he ran the family coach business, he was not conspicuously wealthy. People were quick to point out that under the terms of Lesley's trust, Ronald had much to gain financially from her death.

He faced up to the glare of publicity with fortitude, but in some quarters this was misinterpreted. His stoicism and failure to display his grief in public were seen as sinister self-possession. His position was undermined further when several newspapers ran his photograph alongside one of the Photofits of the Black Panther. By cruel coincidence the likeness was unavoidable. In due course Ronald Whittle received many abusive letters accusing him of his sister's kidnap.

His apparent disagreement with Chief Superintendent Booth – in reality a ruse designed to deceive the kidnapper – also clouded the issue. It had been thought up to convince the Panther that Ronald had not kept the police informed of their abortive rendezvous in Bathpool Park, and that he was committed to paying the ransom money. But Lesley had been dead throughout their deception.

Syndication International

Metropolitan Police

PHOTOFIT EVIDENCE

During the four years Neilson was wanted, police issued six Photofits and several artist's impressions. None led to his capture – he was arrested during a routine check.

The aftermath of the Black Panther case produced more soul-searching among the police than any other mass-murder investigation, except that into the Yorkshire Ripper.

The police investigating the sub-postmaster murders and the Lesley Whittle kidnap had enormous handicaps to cope with, but the inaccurate Photofit pictures still rankle. It was so difficult to recognize Donald Neilson from the Photofit composites, all produced by witnesses who had actually stared him in the face during attacks, that their existence was probably a handicap in the search for the killer.

Artist's image

There was also an artist's impression of the Black Panther, produced after an eight-hour interview with Mr Gerald Smith, the Freightliner security guard who was shot when he disturbed Neilson laying his ransom trail at Dudley, Worcestershire. One of Britain's leading artists produced a painstaking piece of work which, the police were assured by the brave Mr Smith, was an almost exact likeness. Few who have seen Neilson would agree, but the police were not to know that at the time.

All the likenesses emphasized a man with a pinched, almost sharp-featured face, whereas Neilson had quite distinctive round cheeks and an almost boyish face. The artist's impression was the closest likeness, if nothing like as accurate as Mr Smith and the police had hoped.

The Black Panther police even recruited a repertory actor to impersonate the killer in the spring of 1975,

Neilson is unmasked. None of the Photofits or artist's impressions got his hairstyle right.

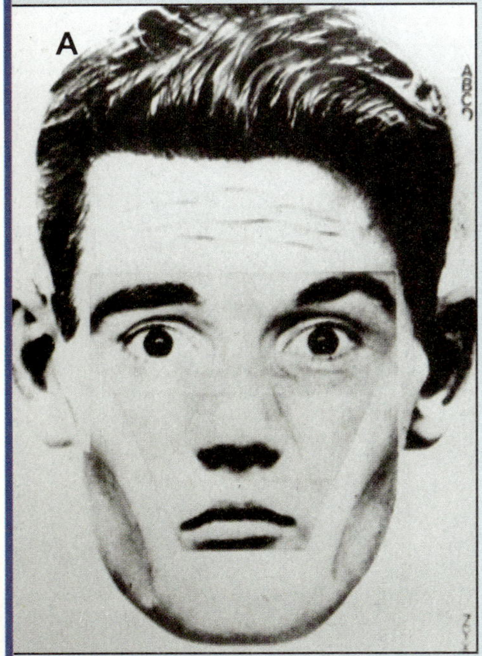

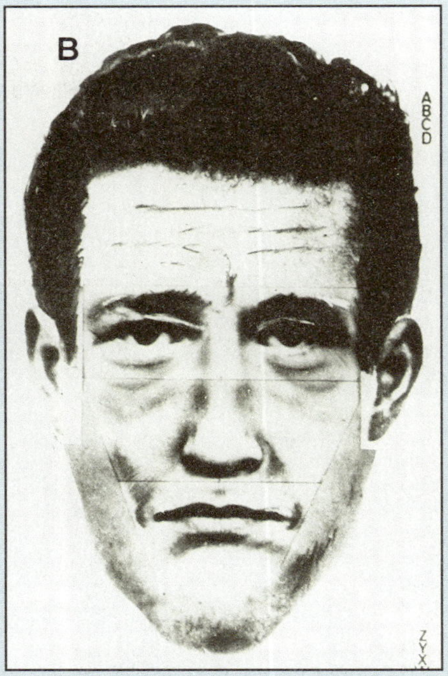

All pictures: Syndication International

but, because he was very similar in appearance to the artist's impression, his reconstruction of events failed to prod the public's memory or produce any new leads.

The presumed advantage of the Photofit system, first introduced in 1970 to replace Identikit, is that it uses real eyes, noses, mouths and other features, rather than the flatter line drawings. Photofit kits contain individual features from photographs filed in criminal records offices. Almost 20 billion faces can be compiled from the complete kit and they are used by police forces throughout the world.

However, the police must also consider the possibility of wasted man hours if an inaccurate image is circulated to newspapers, television and police stations around the country.

David Miller (below), an actor at a Stoke-on-Trent theatre, was made up to resemble the Black Panther. He re-enacted the Panther's movements on the day of the abortive ransom handover.

Yorkshire Post

IDENTIKIT SUCCESS

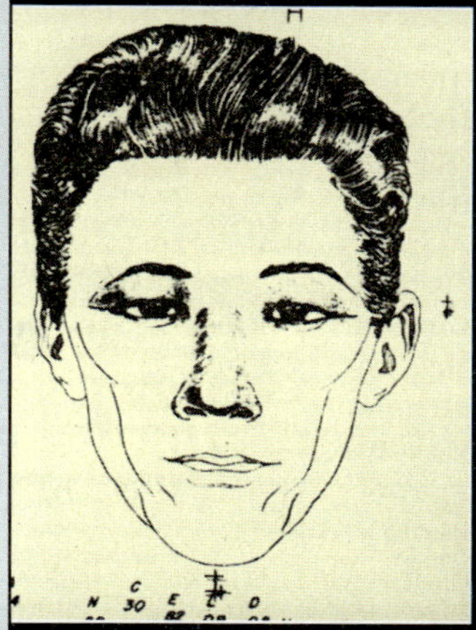

The Identikit system for producing a likeness of a suspect was introduced to Britain from the USA and was first used in London in 1961. The system used a series of transparencies, each of which had a drawing of a facial feature – an eyebrow, nose and so on. A skilled operator could make up a picture from a witness's description.

Identikit scored an early success. On 3 March 1961, an assistant in an antique shop in Cecil Court, London, was stabbed to death. Police obtained descriptions from local shop owners of a man who had been asking about dress swords. The resulting Identikit was circulated to police stations.

Four days later, a constable patrolling nearby Soho saw a man answering the description and detained him for questioning. Subsequent checks produced evidence to convict the suspect, Edwin Bush (above). He confessed and was found guilty.

Photofits, using photos rather than drawings of facial features, were introduced in 1970.

Metropolitan Police

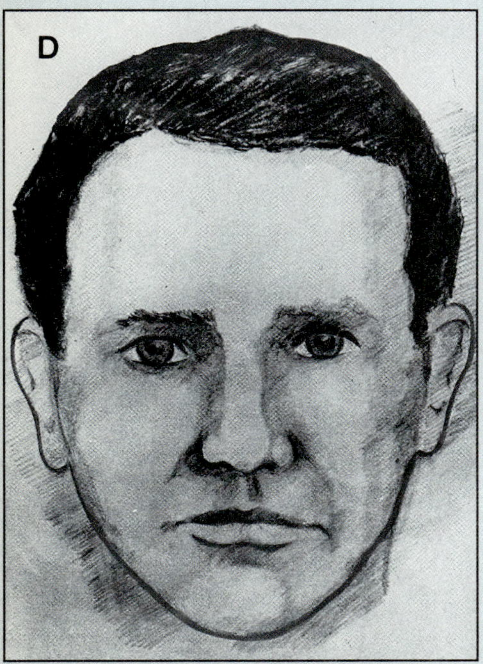

Express & Star, Wolverhampton

Press Association

Five impressions of the Black Panther. The first Photofit A *was from a description by a sub-postmaster who had unmasked Neilson in a struggle on 16 February 1972. The second Photofit* B *was issued in February 1975, and was based on information from witnesses who had seen the Panther as he checked out his phone box ransom trail. The next picture* C *was based on Gerald Smith's description. The drawing* D *– the most accurate – was from information provided by Mrs Grayland, the injured wife of a murdered sub-postmaster.* E *is a cleaned up version of a 1975 sketch which originally showed an unshaven killer in a flat cap.*

Darkest Failure

Lesley Whittle's body was not discovered until seven weeks after her kidnap. But it was to be a further nine months before her kidnapper was finally cornered after a chance confrontation.

The day after Chief Inspector Booth and Ronald Whittle had appeared together on television, the police moved into Bathpool Park, but failed to find any clues. Then two schoolboys came forward with a torch they had found in the park several weeks before. Stuck to the torch was a piece of Dymo tape with the words 'drop suitcase into hole' printed on it. It was clear proof that Ronald Whittle's visit to the park had not been intended as a dry run.

Tragic discovery

On the next day, Friday 7 March, a constable climbed down into the main shaft of the drainage system. Picked out in the light of his torch was the naked body of a young woman suspended from a wire rope near the base of the shaft. On the platform above Lesley Whittle lay a collection of objects.

For those on the investigation it was a shattering blow. 'In my wildest dreams I never dreamed he would do such a thing to the girl. It is terrible,' Booth said afterwards.

Yard in charge

Although the link between the sub-post office murders and the Whittle kidnap had already been made, different investigating teams were working on each of the murders. In order to provide the necessary co-ordination, the head of Scotland Yard's murder squad was put in overall charge of the hunt for the Panther.

A total of 800 police was drafted in to Kidsgrove, where Bathpool Park was situated and every one of the town's 22,000 population was to be interviewed. The murder squad took over Kidsgrove police station, setting up its headquarters there. A special telephone answering machine, known as Robophone, was set up for people who wished to provide information anonymously.

The squad's best hope of tracking down their man lay in the number of items left behind in Bathpool Park. There were clothes, a pair of binoculars, a pencil torch, a flash lamp and a foam mattress identical to the one found in the back of the stolen Morris. One after another, however, these seemingly promising leads turned to dead ends.

A small van owned by a local undertaker (above) waits at the foot of a hill in Bathpool Park as the coffin bearing the body of Lesley Whittle is carried down. A detective displays the wire noose used to kill her (right).

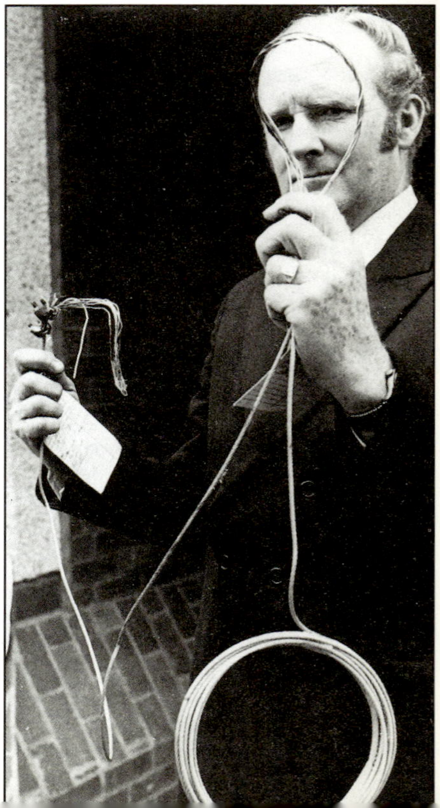

Hulton-Deutsch Collection

KEY DATES

MARCH-DEC 75

7.3.75	Discovery of Lesley Whittle's body
26.4.75	Commander Morrison launches second phase of investigation
11.12.75	Capture of Neilson in Nottinghamshire
13.12.75	Neilson confesses to Lesley Whittle's kidnap

Popperfoto

IN CONTEXT

BAD PUBLICITY

Detective Chief Superintendent Bob Booth, who led the investigation, was severely, but unfairly, criticized in the press for his handling of its opening stages. It was said that Booth should have realized that a kidnap victim's life is most at risk in the 48 hours after abduction, and that he should have had Bathpool Park searched immediately.

Booth, in fact, tried to distance himself from the ransom drops by Ronald Whittle, as a signal to the kidnapper that the police were not involved. Booth hoped this would help to protect Lesley's life. On the day after the first ransom 'drop', Scotland Yard experts did search Bathpool Park, and found nothing suspicious.

The charade was maintained. At one point, Booth and Whittle stage-managed a television appearance in which Whittle said he was interested only in getting his sister back. Booth looked on, irritated and bored. But it was only an act and the officer's motives were misinterpreted.

The binoculars were traced to a shop, where it was found that the purchaser had filled in a guarantee which included a name and address. Police raided the address only to find that it was not a private house but a small commercial company. The name was a false one.

As for most of the other items, their lack of distinguishing marks made it impossible to track them down to a shop, let alone a purchaser.

Many items had been left scattered around Bathpool Park and taken home by people who did not recognize their significance. One man came forward to say that he had found a food hoard near the drainage system. He was able to return saucepans, but

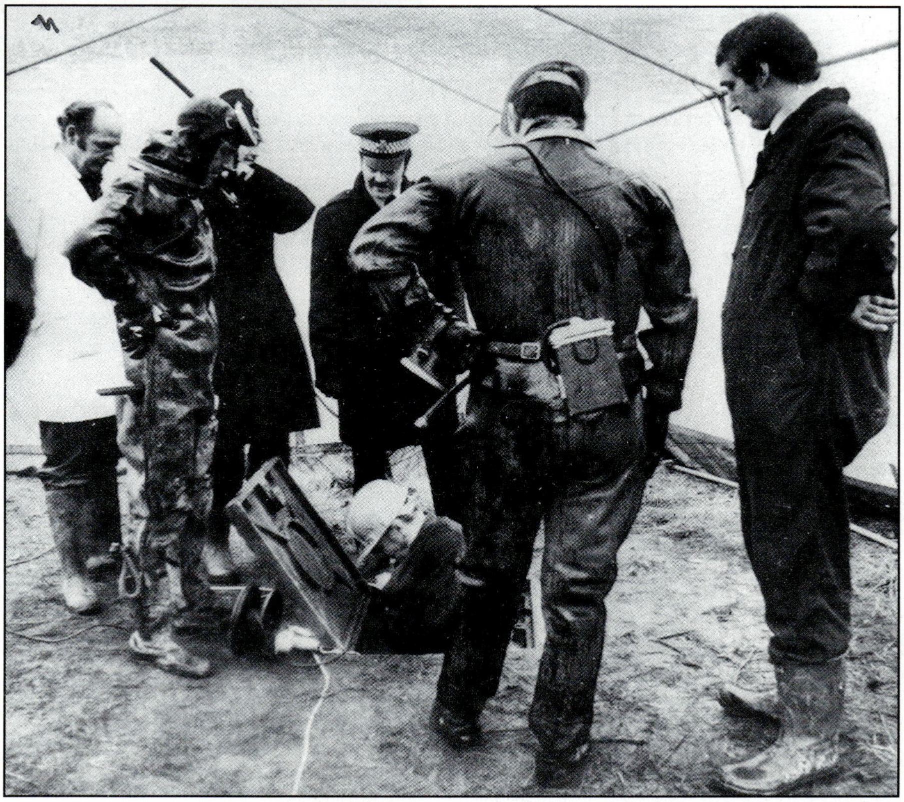

Syndication International

Inside a makeshift tent at Bathpool Park, police frogmen prepare to climb down into the drainage system in search of clues.

IN CONTEXT

PUBLIC HERO

Keith Wood, the man who felled the Black Panther with a single karate blow as Neilson tried to shoot two police officers, had himself once been a suspect in the inquiry. The 41 year-old Wood was standing in the queue at the Junction Chippie, waiting for his regular Friday night supper, when he heard the cry for help from a police car.

Inside, one officer had already been shot. The other was hanging on desperately to the barrels of Neilson's sawn-off shotgun. Wood dragged Neilson out of the car and felled him with a blow to the side of the neck. Another customer at the shop, Roy Morris, helped Wood overpower the small but wiry Neilson, and helped police chain him to some railings nearby. A crowd of about 30 people had gathered.

Wood later disclosed that, six months before, he had been taken by police from his nearby home in Rainworth to Kirby-in-Ashfield police station after his van was reported to have been in Staffordshire at relevant times. Wood was fingerprinted, and questioned for several hours before being cleared of suspicion.

the tinned food had been eaten.

Of more significance was a pocket memo machine, complete with its model and serial number. Nearby, was a broken cassette player and a tape, which when played back was found to have Lesley Whittle's voice on it. Police traced the owners of the memo machines bearing the serial numbers immediately preceding and following that on the one found. But they could make no more progress.

The police found out that postal orders from the post office raids were being cashed in branches throughout the north of England. A news blackout was imposed on this information so that the Panther would carry on cashing them, but because of the volume of postal orders processed by the post offices, his postal orders escaped notice until it was too late.

One of the most complex aspects of the investigation was the decision to interview every person who had been involved in the construction of the Bathpool Park drainage system.

It soon emerged that for each of the three contractors there was a series of sub-contractors who in turn did their own sub-contracting. The scale of this line of inquiry reached almost impossible dimensions. By the end, police were far from sure that they had seen everybody.

The police were also misled by four telephone calls which they mistakenly believed were made by the Panther. They were taken from recordings of incoming calls made at Ronald Whittle's home. The accent belonged to someone from the Black Country and the arrogance of the caller persuaded police it was the Panther.

> **The money, the ransom, was not the most important issue. Freedom at the end of the plan was the most important issue**
>
> DONALD NEILSON

Reconstruction

In an attempt to jog people's memories, a local actor was asked to drive around Kidsgrove in the stolen Morris that had been found near the Freightliner depot. Dressed in clothes similar to the ones that Neilson was known to wear, he stood by telephone boxes and walked around Bathpool Park.

The reconstruction was shown on national television and within 24 hours more than 1,000 telephone calls had been received. Each caller had named people they thought could be the Panther. Everybody who had been named was visited, but Donald Neilson was not among them.

There was another reason why the police were particularly eager to track down the Black Panther. They believed that as long as he remained at large, certain people might be persuaded that kidnap for ransom was a

Express & Star, Wolverhampton

Ronald Whittle (left) on his way to his sister's inquest in Kidsgrove. The pathologist revealed that she had suffered vagal inhibition, meaning she had died either as a result of strangulation or sheer terror.

viable form of crime. And in the wake of the Whittle kidnap, a number of attempted – but unsuccessful – kidnaps did in fact occur.

As 1975 came to an end, the massive and exhaustive police investigation had still not come close to identifying the Black Panther. The one remaining hope for the murder hunt team was that the Panther would come back out into the open and make a mistake.

On Thursday, 11 December, Neilson did just that. At 11 p.m., at Mansfield Woodhouse in Nottinghamshire, two policemen in a parked panda car noticed a suspicious-looking man carrying a hold-all outside the Four Ways pub. The man was Donald Neilson.

Neilson bears the scars (below) from the fight with police and pedestrians during his arrest. The group (right) which overpowered him included (from left) Stuart McKenzie, PC Tony White, PC Roy Morris, and Keith Wood, who delivered the karate chop.

Syndication International

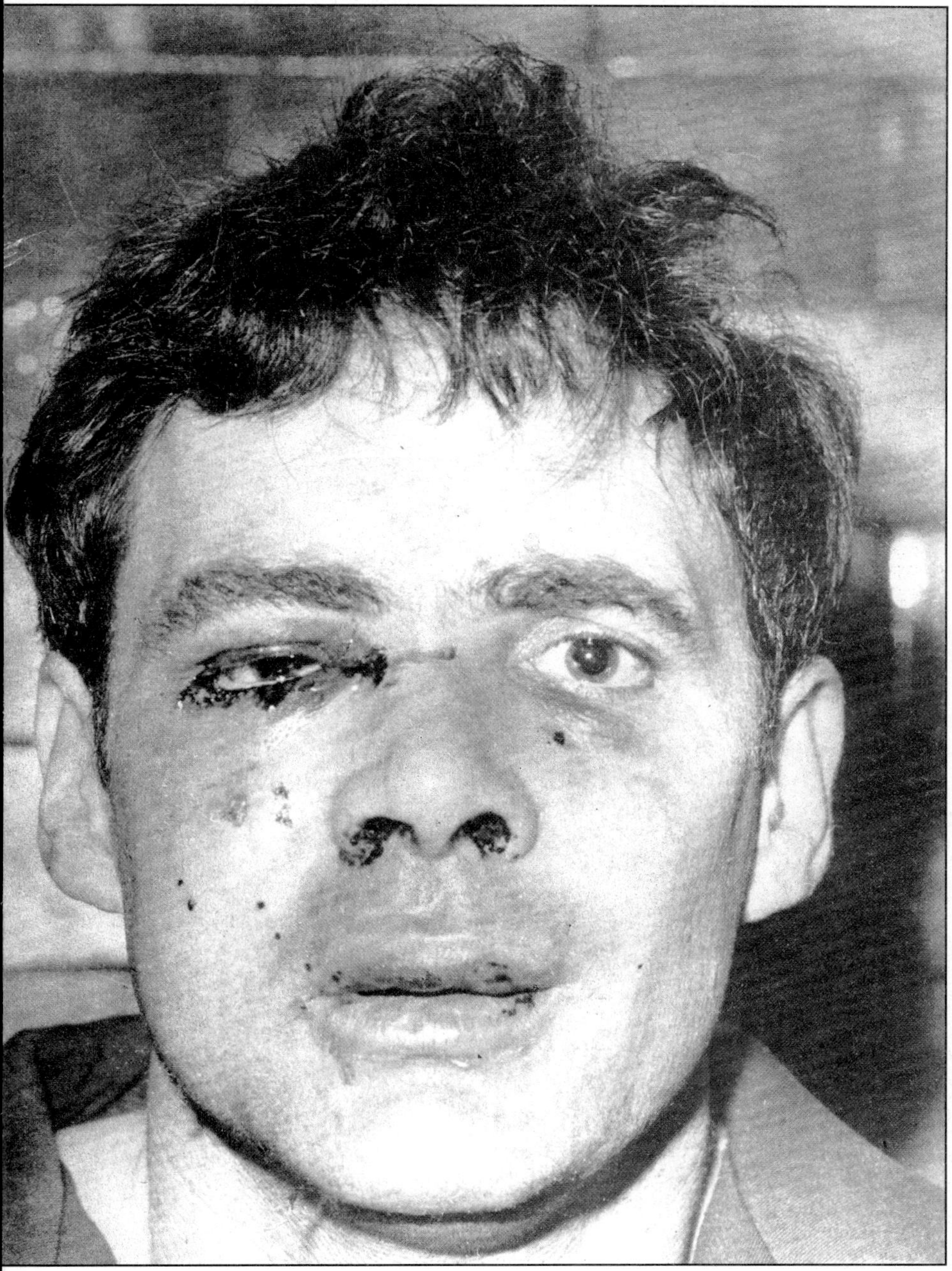

S & G Press Agency

Chance encounter

The two constables – Stuart McKenzie and Tony White – called him over to the car. They asked him for his name and what he had been doing that evening.

Acting friendly, Neilson gave them a false name and said that he was on his way home from work. But when McKenzie asked him to write his name down, Neilson produced a sawn-off shotgun.

Neilson forced PC White into the back of the car and got into the passenger seat. Pressing the shotgun into McKenzie's side, Neilson instructed him to drive to Blidworth, a village six miles away.

As they drove, PC White noticed that for a split second the gun was pointing away from PC McKenzie. White took the opportunity to lunge at Neilson, forcing the muzzle of the gun upwards. As PC McKenzie slammed on the brakes, the shotgun went off into the roof of the car, slightly injuring PC White.

Tackling the Panther

The police car had come to a halt outside a fish and chip shop. As the two policemen grappled with Neilson, two customers rushed over to help them. Neilson struggled and fought with extraordinary strength, but was eventually dragged over to some railings and handcuffed there.

Neilson was driven the 70 miles to Kidsgrove. After 12 hours of questioning, his resistance gave way. He confessed to the kidnap of Lesley Whittle.

A KILLING MACHINE

Neilson's was a psychopathic mind apparently devoid of emotion. But while he could be icily rational, a twisted compulsion drove him to kill.

Donald Neilson was a cunning, devious criminal who displayed all the attributes of a psychopath. His meticulously planned and executed sub-post office raids, and the organization required to carry out the abduction of Lesley Whittle, testify to his ability to think rationally. But at the same time he was prone to panic and acts of senseless savagery.

When he failed to rendezvous with Ronald Whittle to collect the ransom money, he fell into a rage and returned to the hideout to end his victim's life.

Neilson's trail of violence showed that cold-blooded killing did not present him with a psychological or emotional problem. A clue to his behaviour lies in his relatively unloved upbringing, after which he joined the army. His poor record as a soldier demonstrates the problem the psychopath has with learning. He consistently failed to exercise reasonable judgement and was unable to profit by experience. The problem recurred in civilian life when his efforts at making a success of business failed. This is symptomatic of a failure to plan in the longer term. His future in crime was being mapped out at this time.

Paranoid

Following his arrest, Neilson was examined by several psychiatrists and psychologists. All agreed that he was

Express & Star, Wolverhampton

of above average intelligence, psychopathic and obsessional. He was also found to be paranoid about accepting the authority of others, and deeply resentful of those who made more money than he did – which was most people.

There are many well-defined characteristics of the psychopath, but the psychology is still not clearly understood. Although Neilson exhibited many of the traits, he remains a puzzle. It may be said that no sane person kills in the way he did. Yet he was never regarded as legally insane and so was unable to plead diminished responsibility in mitigation of his actions.

Throughout the five weeks of Neilson's two trials, in the sweltering heat of Oxford Crown Court, the man who subjected Lesley Whittle to a hellish world of subterranean caverns and narrow shafts – a world in which he seemed to thrive – showed hardly a flicker of emotion. Sitting rigidly still at the geometrical centre of the airless room, only the top of his head was visible to most of the court. Just once he cracked.

Icy composure

As a recording of Lesley Whittle's tremulous voice echoed round the hushed courtroom, the Black Panther wept openly. By the time he stood to receive several life sentences, Neilson had recovered his icy composure. Turning quickly on his heel, he marched stiffly from the dock and into criminal history as one of Britain's most brutal killers.

THE SOCIOPATH

In the US, the psychopath is often referred to as a sociopath. This description emphasizes the emotional and social emptiness that creates a state of mind capable of abnormally aggressive conduct whose most extreme form may result in murder.

American psychologists have identified a number of characteristics of the sociopath. These include an inability to develop warm, sympathetic relationships, an unstable lifestyle, an inability to accept responsibility for anti-social behaviour, and weak behavioural control. Singly or in combination, such traits may well lead to a life of crime.

Banality of evil: cowed and blanketed, Neilson is led into the murder hunt HQ (left).

During his trial (below), he dressed smartly in suit and tie and remained virtually expressionless throughout.

Syndication International

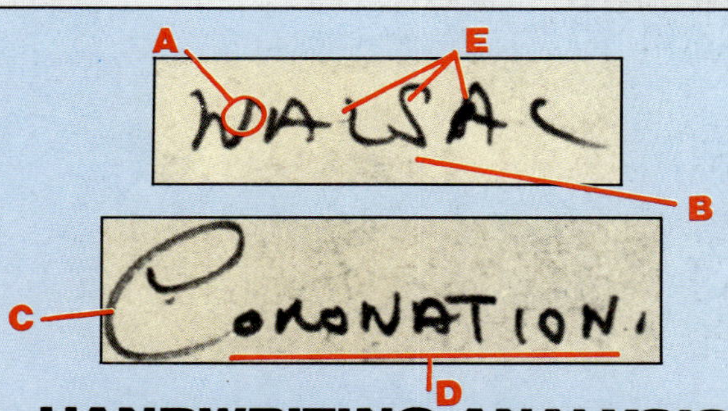

Hulton-Deutsch Collection

HANDWRITING ANALYSIS

The above sample of Neilson's handwriting is dominated by its heavy but uneven pressure and its variation in slant. This suggests that Neilson was easily excited and lacking in emotional equilibrium. He was physically active and liked to be constantly on the move, with a low tolerance of frustration and a primitive need for sensual gratification.

Neilson's script also betrays a need to maintain order and pattern in his life. He was very much a loner and had difficulties in making friends. He is likely to have been the sort of person who was reluctant to acknowledge the achievements of others, yet would have been the first to comment on the least flaw. Inconsistent, changeable and moody, Neilson may well have had parents of contrasting temperaments.

- **A** Spiked 'W': hostile and quick-tempered.
- **B** Heavy, uneven pressure: easily excited and lacking in emotional balance.
- **C** Large capital 'C': exaggerated sense of self-importance.
- **D** Disconnected capitals in words: inclined to act instinctively.
- **E** Slant variation: inconsistent, changeable and easily excited.

James Woodward PO Box 310 London SE20 7RA

FIVE

THE TRIAL

Topham Picture Source

Facing Justice

Donald Neilson admitted to the kidnapping of Lesley Whittle and the three post office shootings, but denied murder on all four counts. As the trial proceeded, however, the weight of evidence began to mount up conclusively against him.

The trial of Donald Neilson began in the sweltering heat of Oxford Crown Court on 14 June 1976. Oxford had been chosen because it was more likely to provide an unprejudiced jury than an area where the Black Panther had operated. The locals seemed unaware that it was taking place, and in scenes untypical of a major murder trial, the streets outside the courtroom were virtually empty.

The scenes inside, however, were electric. Neilson, the ex-soldier, gave an extraordinary performance. He moved in an out of the court marching at the double, holding himself permanently erect. He stood to attention when answering questions, often replying with a snappy 'yes sir' or 'no sir' and all the time staring at a spot high on the window facing the witness box.

> **He was a little man with big ideas. That's the mark of Donald Neilson**
>
> GILBERT GRAY
> Neilson's defence counsel

The basis for Neilson's defence in the Whittle case was that, while he had kidnapped the young heiress, he had not pushed her to her death from the underground ledge. He claimed she had fallen accidentally.

During the Crown's opening speech Neilson took copious notes, and only wavered once, when a tape was played of Lesley Whittle's voice giving the ransom instructions. Neilson, who had prepared for his trial by doing hundreds of press-ups each day, sobbed

Express & Star, Wolverhampton; inset: Metropolitan Police

IN CONTEXT

THE SUSPECT PANDA CAR

A revelation at Neilson's trial was the claim of Chief Superintendent Bob Booth that a blue police panda car had driven through Bathpool Park, with its lights on, during the critical third night of the police surveillance operation. It occurred before Ronald Whittle arrived to deliver the ransom money, and while Donald Neilson was scanning the Park with his binoculars.

Booth had given instructions for all uniformed police to keep out of the vicinity, but the panda car arrived, following the exact route given by the kidnapper and began taking down the numbers of unmarked surveillance vehicles. Booth believed that its presence proved fatal. It was enough to panic Neilson and send him hurrying back to the drainage shaft, where he murdered Lesley Whittle and made his escape.

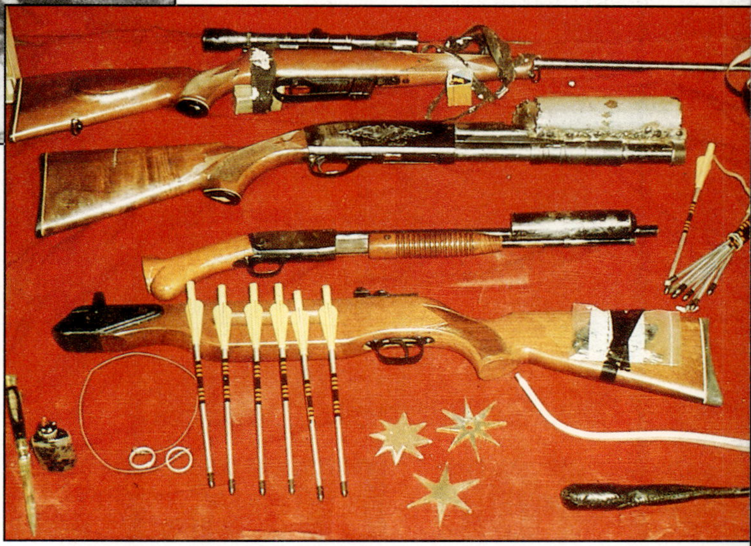

Under a blanket, Neilson (above) is taken for committal. To accommodate press and public, Kidsgrove's Victoria Hall was used rather than the smaller magistrate's court. The weapons (right) were part of Neilson's formidable arsenal.

into a handkerchief.

Neilson claimed that he had always planned to release Lesley Whittle. The Crown countered this by suggesting that it had been Neilson's intention from the very first day to kill her. While Neilson maintained that she had never seen his face throughout her ordeal, the Crown reminded him of his own evidence, when he talked of her seeing a look of alarm on his face at one point.

'If she had seen your face,' Phillip Cox, for the prosecution said, 'she would recognize your face on a subsequent occasion and you could not have allowed her to live.'

Military precision

Neilson seemed to have an idea that if he explained everything sensibly, in a matter of fact manner, and with his favourite military precision, then the jury would understand and realize it had all been a ghastly mistake, a master plan that had gone wrong for the right reasons. He rarely looked the jury's way. If he had, he would have detected the open-mouthed revulsion among several of them as he attempted to make Lesley Whittle's journey from the safety of her home to the Bathpool Park drainage system seem ordinary.

Before leaving her in the shaft, Neilson had tethered her. He said she

KEY DATES

MARCH-JULY 76

30.3.76	Neilson's committal
14.6.76	Neilson's trial begins at Oxford Crown Court
21.6.76	DCS Bob Booth gives evidence
21.7.76	Neilson sentenced to life imprisonment

had made no comment when he had placed the wire noose over her head. She had not objected when he took off her dressing gown so she could dry herself with it. He even explained to the court how the police, in his opinion, would have been wise to recruit two SAS men to help track him down. He had, after all, been training for the kidnap for three years.

Tortured logic

Neilson then explained the third night in Bathpool Park, when he had flashed his torch at the wrong car when Ronald Whittle had arrived late. Looking increasingly desperate, Neilson took 34 minutes of tortured logic to explain just how and why Lesley Whittle had died. His voice rose and fell, his eyes blazed and he looked close to losing control, particularly when the Crown insisted that he had no option but to kill Lesley when his plan had gone wrong.

One of the most compromising pieces of evidence was the Dymo tape with the words 'police or tricks – death' printed on it. Neilson was adamant that it was a threat he did not intend to carry out. In the same way, he changed the emphasis of his evidence, saying the ransom money was secondary to his escape.

When Neilson was questioned ab-

Express & Star, Wolverhampton

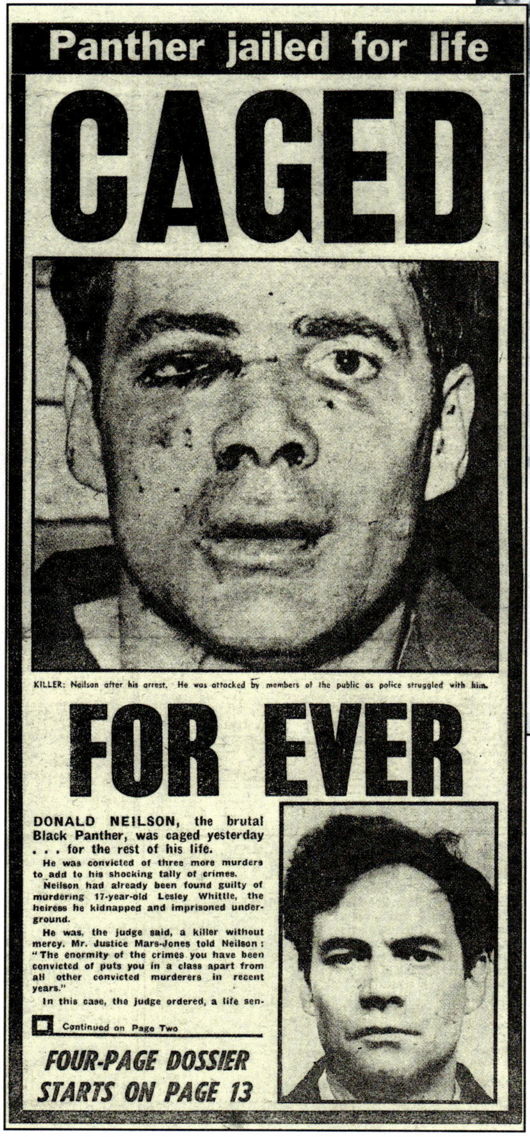

Panther jailed for life

CAGED

KILLER: Neilson after his arrest. He was attacked by members of the public as police struggled with him.

FOR EVER

DONALD NEILSON, the brutal Black Panther, was caged yesterday . . . for the rest of his life.

He was convicted of three more murders to add to his shocking tally of crimes.

Neilson had already been found guilty of murdering 17-year-old Lesley Whittle, the heiress he kidnapped and imprisoned underground.

He was, the judge said, a killer without mercy. Mr. Justice Mars-Jones told Neilson: "The enormity of the crimes you have been convicted of puts you in a class apart from all other convicted murderers in recent years."

In this case, the judge ordered, a life sen-

Continued on Page Two

FOUR-PAGE DOSSIER STARTS ON PAGE 13

Syndication International/John Frost Newspapers

Mr Gilbert Gray, QC (above), Neilson's defence counsel, successfully argued that the charges of shooting Gerald Smith and attempted murder of PC McKenzie should be heard at a separate hearing.
Neilson was tried first for kidnapping Lesley Whittle, demanding a ransom and murdering her. The popular press (left) supported the judge's final sentence.